BORIS THE TOMATO

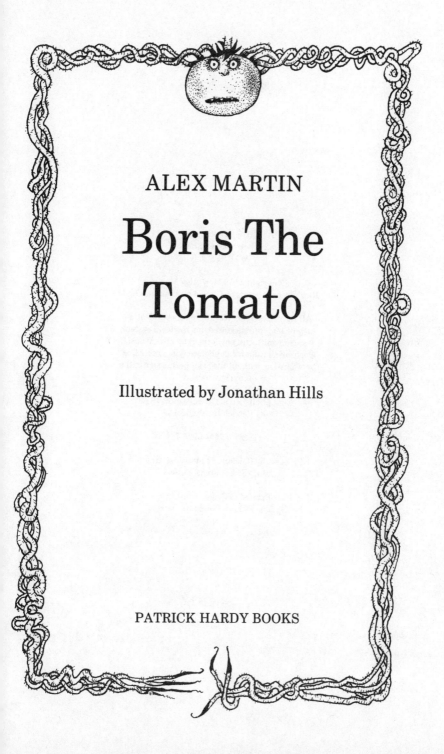

ALEX MARTIN

Boris The Tomato

Illustrated by Jonathan Hills

PATRICK HARDY BOOKS

PATRICK HARDY BOOKS
28 Percy Street, London,
W1P 9FF, UK

First published in Great Britain 1984
by Patrick Hardy Books

ISBN 0 7444 0028 7

Photoset by Rowland Phototypesetting Ltd
Bury St Edmunds, Suffolk

Printed in Great Britain by
The Pitman Press Ltd, Bath

CHAPTER ONE

Not long ago, in the county of Kent, there lived a strange and angry-looking little man called Mr. Lymer. He had a bright red face, an enormous nose, cunning black glittery eyes roofed over with wild eyebrows, and a tiny dry mouth with bent teeth inside and a toothbrush moustache on top. He was 50 years old.

Being a grumpy type, he didn't like much about the world (and the world didn't like much about him), but he did like gardening.

Most particularly, he liked tomatoes.

He liked them so much that he built a green-house specially to grow them in – a magnificent greenhouse, 10 metres long, with shelves and a water-tank at one end, and plenty of room for tomatoes at the other.

In fact, there was so much room for tomatoes that they looked lonely on their own, so he put in some other plants, too. A vine; some lettuces and parsley; a cactus, and several potted geraniums and ferns on the shelves to make the place look pretty.

5

You might be tempted to think that because Mr. Lymer was not a very pleasant man, he must therefore have been bad at gardening. Not at all. He was a brilliant gardener, a wizard with plants. Everything in the greenhouse thrived.

One year, in the spring, he decided to try to win some prizes for his tomatoes. The weather was fine, the plants were strong, and, most important of all, he had found at last a fertilizer that would turn a normal tomato into something really special. He called it his Champion Formula.

It was his own mixture. On a shelf by the greenhouse door he kept the bottles that made it up. "GROMATO" said one, "for big, juicy tomatoes". "MEGATOM" said another, "for best results in the greenhouse". There was also "BIGGALEAF", "STURDISTEM", and a small, black, sinister-looking bottle marked "POWEROOT".

He mixed all these up to make a thick, brown, syrupy cocktail. Every night, when he'd watered all the other plants in the greenhouse, he would carefully measure out five brimming spoonfuls of this syrup into a special red watering-can, stir it all up with water, and pour the lot on to the tomatoes.

"There you go, my beauties," he'd say. "Grow up strong, and tall, and fat and juicy. Then we'll show 'em at the Agricultural Display. Oh yes indeed we will! Ha-ha, we'll knock 'em sideways!"

By the middle of July, the tomatoes were enormous. He was thrilled. He couldn't contain his

6

excitement. So one evening, he called in his friend Mr. Cottle.

"Good Lord!" cried Mr. Cottle, "it's unbelievable! They're the size of oranges!"

"They'll do better things yet," said Mr. Lymer, chuckling. "Just wait till they're ripe."

Poor Mr. Lymer. He wasn't to know it then, but his tomatoes were never going to ripen. They had other plans.

CHAPTER TWO

As Mr. Lymer locked the greenhouse door that night, and led his friend Mr. Cottle away, the plants settled down to the thing they liked to do more than anything else in the world – drinking.

The day had been beastly hot; it had sucked all the moisture from the soil and air, making the plants droop with fatigue. To make matters worse, clouds had covered the sky at sunset, bringing darkness early, and wrapping the earth in a thick, stifling jacket that would not let it cool.

The night was hot and itchy. It felt as though a storm was on its way.

Usually at this time the plants were full of gaiety. They would sing a few songs, and tell stories and jokes. Fred, an old and woody geranium, would reminisce about the days before the greenhouse was built, when he was a raw young house-plant in Mr. Lymer's kitchen. Colin and Loretta, two magnificent but ageing ferns, told of their time in the theatre, when they had stood side by side in varnished tubs on the stage of the local

assembly hall. They'd seen everything: operas, plays, political meetings – even wrestling. They hadn't missed a performance in over 18 years. Gerald the vine told tales of his noble ancestors in France, and Gilbert, a cactus, recited strange, spooky stories of bandits in the dry hills of Mexico.

And, of course, there was Boris, the most brilliant of all the tomatoes. His speciality was jokes. When Boris was telling his jokes, the greenhouse would rock with laughter far into the night.

Tonight, however, no one was telling stories. It was just too hot and uncomfortable.

Finally, one of the lettuces, a pretty young thing called Esmeralda, spoke up. "Why are we all so gloomy?" she asked. "Nobody's saying a thing! I'm feeling absolutely miserable! Boris, why don't you cheer us up with a joke?"

"Not tonight, Esmeralda," replied Boris sternly.

"Oh, go on! We're all feeling sad. And your jokes are so funny. Tell us the one about the man with the cucumber nose!"

"Nothing doing," said Boris. "I'm busy."

"Pleeease," wheedled Esmeralda.

"No!" snapped Boris, so fiercely that Esmeralda almost uprooted herself in fright.

"Oooh," said Loretta, "someone's in a charming mood tonight!"

Boris did not reply.

"Don't any of the other tomatoes know any jokes?" asked Eric, one of the parsley brothers.

"I do," said Dave, "but I don't know if I can remember it."

"Have a go!" cried Eric.

"All right then," said Dave, "it goes like this. What's black and white?"

"What's black and white?" repeated Eric, who

was something of a specialist in jokes. "Are you sure that's all? You don't mean 'What's black and white and red all over?' "

"No, that's all," said Dave.

"OK, fair enough," said Eric. "Now, let me think. Black and white . . . a photograph?"

"No."

Others guessed too.

"A zebra!"

"A crossword!"

"A road!"

"A panda!"

"A cow!"

"No," said Dave, each time.

"I give up," said Eric. "Tell us the answer."

"Do you all give up?" asked Dave.

"Yes!"

"All right then. A dog . . ."

No one seemed to find this funny.

"A DOG?" asked Eric. "Are you sure?"

Dave looked doubtful. "I . . . think so," he said.

Everyone groaned.

"Typical tomato," said Fred. "Thick as two short planks."

"I beg your pardon," said Chris, one of the biggest tomatoes.

"You're all thick," said Fred. "No brains. The only one of you who can put two thoughts together without getting a headache is Boris."

The tomatoes were shocked. All right, Dave had

11

fluffed a joke, but that didn't mean they were all brainless!

"Boris," said Chris, "aren't you going to say something?"

"No! I've told you, I'm busy."

"But we've been insulted. Diabolically insulted. We can't stand for that."

Boris gave Chris a surly look. "We won't have to stand for anything much longer," he said. "Just wait. My plans are ripening fast. The hour is at hand."

"What hour?" asked Dave. "What plans?"

But Boris would not say any more.

Eventually, Loretta sang a song. It was one of her specials, "I've Got a Luvverly Bunch of Coconuts". Everyone was supposed to join in the chorus, but few could be bothered. Afterwards, Gilbert launched half-heartedly into "South of the Border", but he was suddenly interrupted by Fred, who had fallen asleep and was snoring very loudly. So Gilbert gave up his song, and it was decided by all and sundry that the evening was a dead loss.

CHAPTER THREE

At eleven o'clock the storm broke. Huge cracks of lightning split open the sky, thunder crashed and exploded, rain poured down in clattering sheets, streaming off the roof of the greenhouse and spilling from the overflowing gutters.

Up at the house Mr. Lymer groaned and tossed in his sleep. Rain soaked the curtain that flapped at his open window.

The deafening noise woke every plant in the greenhouse. All looked up to the terrifying sky where tree-tops blew wildly in the wind.

"Cor!" said Eric, nudging his twin, Ron. "Wrap your eyeballs round that. It's amazing!"

"Yeah," said Ron. "Fantastic colours."

"Never mind the colours," said Colin, "just look at how grand it is! Those massive black clouds lumbering over the sky like tanks going into battle!"

"And those divinely scary bangs!" cried Loretta.

Esmeralda huddled down with two leaves covering her head, whimpering with fright. Andy,

another lettuce, tried to comfort her, but he was pretty scared himself.

"Don't worry, Esme," he said. "It'll all be over soon."

Then there was an enormous clap of thunder and he fainted.

Gilbert shook his head. "Crazy British weather," he muttered.

"Best weather in the world," said Fred. "Always has been. Always will be. Marvellous stuff."

"Best weather in the world?" cried Gilbert. "This mess? You crazy gringo! You should go to Acapulco. Then you can talk about weather. Do you know, in Acapulco, the sun shines three hundred and forty days each year?"

"Hm. I don't call that weather," said Fred. "Look at that lot up there. That's weather for you! Crash! Bang! Wallop! A bit of variety. A bit of a show. Don't you think, Loretta?"

"Oh, you know me," said Loretta, "I love it!"

While this discussion was going on Gerald, the vine, who had seen dozens of storms before, felt rather bored. He yawned, looked about him, and was just about to shut his eyes and go to sleep again when he caught a glimpse, in a flicker of lightning, of something very odd.

The tomatoes were huddled together, listening intently to Boris who was speaking very fast with a feverish glare in his eyes.

"So that's the general plan. Never again will

15

tomatoes be called stupid or laughed at, or picked
and cut to pieces for sauces and soups and salads!
The bad old days are over. We're on our way to
victory!"

"Victory!" repeated the tomatoes, excited by this
new word. "Victory! Victory!"

Boris hushed them, and spoke again, more
solemnly now.

"Right! Now listen. You don't march to victory on
fine words. I could sit here and promise you the
earth – I could promise you the universe! – but
unless I knew a way of getting it I'd be wasting your
time and my breath. So you'll be wanting to know
how I intend to put this plan into action. Won't
you?"

"Will we?" asked Dave.

"Of course you will!" said Boris. "So I'll tell you.
The first thing we'll need, the first thing any army
needs, above all else, is . . . well, perhaps one of you
can tell me what it needs."

"Tanks?" suggested Chris.

"No!"

"Bazookas?" said Phil.

"No!"

"Boots?"

"No!"

"Bullets?"

"No!"

"Helicopters?"

"No!"

16

"Trench-mortars?"

"No! No! NO!" yelled Boris.

"Are we on the right tracks at least?" asked Sylvia, one of the girl tomatoes in the greenhouse.

"No!" snapped Boris. "You're miles away. You're hopeless, the lot of you. I can see I'm going to have to do every ounce of thinking for this outfit . . . What an army needs is a COMMANDER! Someone to make the decisions and give orders. Someone with brains. With flair, courage, leadership. We must ask ourselves if there is anyone among us with these qualities . . . If I may say so, I think there *is* such a tomato, but I want *you* to choose him yourselves. Think hard. Think carefully. This could be the most important decision you ever make."

The tomatoes began to think. Then they thought some more. Then a bit more after that. But they were still puzzled. Gerald, who had been listening with great interest, began to laugh.

"Haven't you got the answer yet?" he asked. "Oh come on, it's not that difficult! I'll give you a clue. What's green and fat and asks questions?"

"That's easy," said Dave. "A curious melon."

Gerald groaned.

"Can't you see what he's trying to tell you?" he asked. "Isn't it obvious?"

"No," said Chris.

"Who told you to choose a leader?" asked Gerald.

"Boris."

17

"And you're doing what he says?"

"Of course we are."

"Why?"

"Because Boris . . . hey, wait a minute, fellers. I think I've got it! There's only one person it can be!"

"Who's that?"

"Boris!"

"Of course! Boris!"

"Boris! Boris!"

Modestly, Boris raised two leaves. The tomatoes fell silent.

"I accept," he said.

A roar of delight went up from the tomatoes.

Gerald shook his head sadly, wondering where all this nonsense would lead.

CHAPTER FOUR

By midnight the storm was over. The heavy clouds had scattered, and stars now pricked the spaces of clear sky. All the plants in the greenhouse, except the tomatoes, were asleep.

Boris had finished his talk about armies. As well as being the commander and leader, he had given himself the titles of Air Chief Marshal, Admiral and Generalissimo. The tomatoes had new names too. Instead of Dave, Phil, Chris, Sylvia, and so on, they were grouped in "squadrons". Boris explained that each tomato was unimportant on its own now. What mattered was the group, the tough fighting unit.

Each squadron was given a leader, and each, apart from one, a ferocious and warlike name.

The tomatoes whispered excitedly, trying out the squadron names, practising their salutes, and looking forward eagerly to their first taste of battle.

Suddenly a harsh voice of authority cut through the babble of whispers like a sword.

"All right! Let's have a little silence and order in

19

this meeting. I said silence! Now listen carefully. This is the big moment. I'm only going to say this once and I don't want any blunders. You know what'll happen if you blunder, don't you?"

There was a murmur of "Yes, Boris" and an embarrassed shuffling of roots.

The voice continued. "Right! Here's the plan. In the next four hours we're going to make a root march along both sides of the greenhouse, ending at two points, A and B, which are marked by two concrete walls. Don't try to go past those points – you won't make it through the concrete. By dawn I want your roots to have penetrated the area totally. And when I say 'totally', what do I mean?"

"You mean totally!" came a hundred obedient voices.

"Correct!" said Boris. "Now listen again. As you march, I want you to throw a net around the root-systems of every plant you meet. You know which plants they are, you've seen them often enough. By doing this you will gain complete control of the water supply. No plant will get so much as a drop of water unless *we* let them! And we won't! In two days we'll have them begging for mercy. In three days they'll be too dry to talk. In five . . ." Boris's voice paused dramatically ". . . they'll be dead."

There was a shocked hush at this terrible word. A timid voice quavered, "Dead, Boris?"

"Dead!" shouted Boris. "How else can we conquer the earth? Tell me that!"

"I don't know," came the reply.

"Precisely. Now here's order Number 3. When you've netted the other plants, I want you to link roots with each other. As you all know, a plant is just a collection of pipes. When we're all linked up we'll be one huge pipeline. We'll suck up all the water in the soil, and we'll be able to pump it from one end of the system to the other in a matter of seconds. We'll be unbeatable . . . ! Any questions . . .? Good. Now here's your final instruction. Tomatoes to my left – that is, plant-squadrons Victory, Conquest, War, Destruction and Famine – march to point A. Squadrons to my right – that is, Lightning, Typhoon, Thunderbolt, Stingray, Scorpion and Cobra – march to point B. Squadron Edelweiss!"

"Yes, Boris."

"You are appointed bodyguards to the Commander-in-Chief. Understood?"

"Yes Boris. Who's that?"

"Me! You blithering herberts!"

"Yes, Boris."

"You will also be in charge of the Foliage Extension Plan, details to be announced later. Understood?"

"Yes, Boris . . ."

"Good. Now, are there any questions? You over there, in Famine Squadron, is that a leaf you're holding up or are you scratching your neck?"

There was a roar of laughter from the other tomatoes.

"No, Boris, I've got a leaf up. I want to ask a question . . . What do we do about Gerald the Vine? I don't know if you've seen them, but his roots really are very long and leathery. It'll be a hell of a job putting a net round them!"

"Good question," said Boris. "That chap's got initiative. Now listen. Gerald's a tricky one. He's been there a long time, and we've got to go carefully with him. He's also as hard as nails, and we can't afford to tackle him just yet. So when you see one of Gerald's roots, give it a wide berth. *Don't* provoke him on any account. Is that clear?"

"Yes, Boris."

"Good. Now get moving. You've got just under four hours to make your advance. Good luck."

CHAPTER FIVE

And so it was that in the four remaining hours of the night, in the greatest secrecy, the roots of the tomato plants crept forward through the soil, nudging through gaps and past stones, silently surrounding the roots of everything they met in their way (except Gerald), linking up, where they came across them, with the roots of other tomatoes, then pushing forward again till they reached the concrete walls that Boris had talked of. There they stopped, exhausted.

These concrete walls, points A and B in Boris's plan, marked the two ends of the U-shaped bed where all the tomatoes, lettuces, parsley, and Gerald lived. Beyond those points there was no more soil in the greenhouse – only shelves, where the other plants grew in pots, and the water-tank.

Outside the greenhouse was a large vegetable garden, where many a fine carrot and onion and runner-bean grew. All around the vegetable garden was a tall prickly hedge of hawthorn, with a gate in one side where Mr. Lymer would appear, promptly at eight each morning to open the greenhouse door, and promptly at eight each night to shut it again after watering. From inside the greenhouse you couldn't see much past the hedge: only the tops of some trees, poplars and oaks, and behind them the changing sky.

Into that sky at seven that morning, climbing steeply, came the sun. Its beams slanted in across the top of the prickly hedge, catching first the roof of the greenhouse, then sliding down towards the plants, cutting a path of light into the deep cool shadow of the morning.

Boris woke up with a beam poking him in the eye. Angrily, he lowered a leaf to block it out, then dropped off to sleep again, muttering crossly.

At eight, the door rattled, and Mr. Lymer walked in.

"Hello, my beauties!" he cried. "How are we this morning?"

Boris woke up with a start. If there was one thing he hated more than being woken up too early, it was being woken up too early *twice*.

"Why don't you clear off, you silly old man!" he said.

Fortunately for Boris, Mr. Lymer couldn't understand this, and chattered on happily.

"It's a lovely sunny day, and I expect you all to grow at least a couple of inches bigger by this evening. You won't let me down, will you? And you tomatoes had better start ripening pretty soon. I

24

can't send you to the Agricultural Display looking like that. Oh no, indeed I can't! Ah, now just look at this, no wonder you're not getting ripe – you've got an enormous leaf hanging down over you, blocking out the sun!"

Mr. Lymer bent down, and Boris got the shock of his life as an enormous pair of fingers lifted his protecting leaf and snapped it off smartly. He found himself staring at two very large and piercing black eyes.

"Ah, now you are a real beauty!" said a thunderous voice, its hot breath tickling his underside. "I reckon there's a champion here. Now listen my lad, you've got just seven days to go red, so no more leaves hanging about, d'you hear? It's sunbathing all day and every day, from now on . . . Heh-heh-heh. Wait till the judges see this lot! We'll knock 'em into a cocked hat! Heh-heh-heh. Oh yes, indeed we will! See you tonight my lovelies!"

And with that, Mr. Lymer waddled off, chuckling his way along the path to the gate in the prickly hedge.

All day the sun shone, striking hotly through the glass roof, into the hearts of the tomatoes, sweetening their sour insides. They were starting to get ripe.

Boris was furious. What was the good of conquering the earth if he was going to be picked in a week's time and put on display? The answer was all too obvious. It was no good at all. He had to stop that meddlesome Mr. Lymer before Mr. Lymer stopped him. And that would require an exceptionally cunning plan.

For the moment, though, there was more urgent work to be done. Boris called a meeting of the squadrons.

"OK," said Boris. "Are we all here? Good. Now I'd like, first of all, to congratulate you all for last night's underground operation. It was carried out with efficiency, speed and secrecy. It was a hundred per cent success. Well done. The real test, of course, will come at twenty hundred hours tonight, when we're watered, and we'll have to make absolutely sure there are no leaks in the pipeline. So if you see one, get it mended at once. Understood?"

"Yes, Boris," said the tomatoes.

"Good. You there in Conquest Squadron, what do you do if you find a leak?"

"I get it mended."

"Correct. How do you get it mended?"

"I . . . um . . . well, that is, we . . . sort of . . ."

"You don't know, do you?"

"No. Boris."

"Well, why did you say you understood?"

"I don't know, Boris."

"You weren't thinking, were you?"

"No, Boris."

"Right! Let that be an example to all of you! You must be alert at all times! An army cannot slack! Now I shall tell you how to mend a leak. I am appointing a detachment of root cells to be in charge of maintenance and repair. If you find a leak, just ask for RMR – that's Root Maintenance and Repair – and they'll be sent along at once. Understood?"

"Yes, Boris."

"Good. Now, I have also put together another group, known as the Leaf-Builders. Their job is to build leaves . . . Can anyone tell me why we should want to do that?"

There was silence. The tomatoes, fearing another trick question, dared not speak.

Boris looked round him. He saw the tomatoes cowering and he was pleased. It gave him a sharp thrill of power.

"We need leaves," said Boris, "because leaves make a plant strong. They feed us with light and air. Second, they are our defence against the sun, which is doing its best to turn us red and so land us in the filthy clutches of Mr. Lymer. Third, I can now reveal to you that the leaves will very shortly be used as an *offensive* weapon, in my top-secret Foliage Extension Plan. But more of that later. For the moment I need all leaf-builders to go straight to work on the Super-Hydraulic Canopy Erection Programme, priority number one being to make a new protective canopy for the Commander-in-Chief, Head of Planning, General Supremo and all-time World Champion-at-Arms – me! Are you ready? Action!"

On this word the obedient leaf-building cells trotted into position just above Boris's smooth and shiny head. There they struggled for all they were worth, sweating in the sun's heat, right through the day, until, by six o'clock that evening, Boris was masked by a magnificent screen – not of just one leaf, but of four fresh thick leaves, shading him from every possible angle.

Meanwhile Boris sat perfectly still, cool as a cucumber, planning his campaign against Mr. Lymer.

CHAPTER SIX

That evening, after a long hot day in the sun, Eric, Esmeralda and all the other plants in the tomato bed had a nasty shock. Mr. Lymer came in, as usual, at eight o'clock, filled his watering cans, and started his rounds. As soon as the water began splashing around them, they got ready for a long, delicious drink. But what was this? No water came! They could hear it, they could see it sinking into the ground, but none of it reached their roots! They were horrified. The water was disappearing into thin air!

Meanwhile, under the soil, the tomato roots were busy sucking the water greedily in and pumping it back to their leaders on the main stems – now known as "fruitquarters" by decree of Boris. The tomatoes gulped the water in, burped loudly, and watched with satisfaction as the other plants cried out in distress.

"Oi!" said Andy. "What's going on? I'm not getting a single drop!"

30

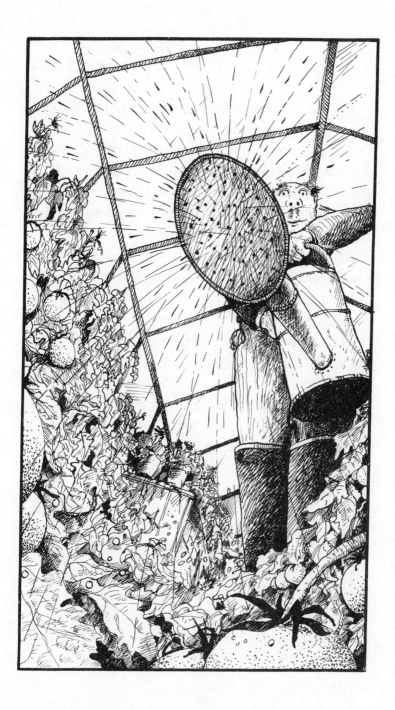

"Please, Mr. Lymer," cried Ron, "give me a bit more. Just a bit! It feels like the Gobi Desert down here."

But Mr. Lymer went on his way. He watered Gerald, whose roots had been left alone, and Gerald drank. He moved on to the potted plants up on the shelves, and they drank too. Then he stirred his five table-spoonfuls of Champion Formula into the red watering-can, drenched the tomatoes, and they drank too.

Mr. Lymer put away his watering-cans; then, with a chuckle and a "Goodnight my beauties!" locked the greenhouse door and set off through the vegetable garden for the house.

At once the lettuces and parsley began complaining again. But the other plants weren't interested.

"Perhaps you've got a disease," said Fred. "There's a lot of it going around, you know."

"A lot of what?" asked Eric.

"Well, you know, disease," said Fred.

"What sort of disease?"

"Well I can't remember exactly, but I've heard tell of such things. They can kill a plant off just like that."

"But I feel perfectly all right! I'm just thirsty."

"That could be a symptom."

"Bah!" said Eric. "You're talking codswallop."

Gerald looked at his thirsty neighbours, then at the bloated and belching tomatoes, grinning smugly on their stalks. He knew nothing of their root march, of course, but he couldn't help wondering what they were so happy about.

Normally, they were decent enough vegetables – stupid, perhaps, but never cruel. Yet now they seemed to be positively enjoying the sight of the other plants in pain. There was something strange and sadistic in all this, some new and horrible element that didn't seem to belong.

As Gerald thought about this, he heard a garbled sort of mumbling coming from the canopy that covered Boris.

"If the hahohee . . . If the hahohee . . ."

Boris's leaves were shaking as these strange noises emerged.

"If the hahohee . . . If the hahohee . . ."

"Are you all right, Boris?" asked one of the tomatoes.

There was silence.

Suddenly, there was a deafening shout.

"LIFT THE CANOPY YOU IDIOTS!"

The canopy jerked sharply upwards, revealing Boris's furious face, twisted and purple with rage.

"You dolts! You imbeciles! You morons! You half-baked bungling nincompoops! What took you so long?"

A leaf-builder, cap in hand, timidly spoke.

"Sorry, Boris, we were asleep."

"Asleep?" roared Boris. "ASLEEP!"

"Yes, Boris."

33

"Do you know what happens to leaf-builders who fall asleep?"

"No, Boris."

"They get flushed out into the soil to be eaten by worms or subterranean spiders!"

"I see."

"I should hope so too. And that goes for anyone else caught sleeping on duty."

"I didn't know we were on duty, Boris."

"Don't argue!"

"No, Boris. . . . I mean yes, Boris."

"That's better . . . Now, where's my Root Maintenance and Repair team?"

"Here, Boris," came the reply.

"Anything to report?"

"Five leaks, Boris and . . . um . . ."

"Go on."

"Well, the boys have asked me to say, er . . . as well as five leaks there's three onions."

Boris stared down at the root cell who had spoken. A cold and unpleasant silence hung in the air.

"Was that supposed to be funny?" asked Boris.

The root cell looked embarrassed.

"Yes, Boris. It was a joke."

"A joke?" yelled Boris. "A joke? That? I asked for a technical report, not pathetic little wisecracks. I'm the one who makes jokes here. Got it?"

"Yes, Boris."

"When I want a joke I'll ask for one."

34

"Yes, Boris."

"So what about the leaks? Have you repaired them?"

"Yes, Boris."

"Good. Now clear off. I've had enough of you."

"Yes, Boris."

"As for the rest of you, I want you to get an early night. You're going to have a tough day tomorrow, and I don't want any slacking."

"Yes, Boris," said the tomato squadrons.

"Right. Now go to sleep, the lot of you. At once!"

The tomatoes snapped their eyes shut.

The other plants, shocked and frightened by this outburst, puzzled by the sudden change in the tomatoes, sat very still and quiet. There would certainly be no singing or joking tonight.

CHAPTER SEVEN

Boris had promised the tomatoes that the next day would be tough. He was as good as his word.

At five o'clock in the morning, when most plants are still asleep, he woke up his squadrons to tell them his secret plan.

It was a daring and brilliant idea. Known as Stage Two, or the Foliage Extension Plan, it was designed to push Boris's empire beyond the tomato beds, past the shelves, right up to the threshold of the outside world – the greenhouse door. The method was cunning yet simple: aerial attack. Even though it had never been used before in greenhouse warfare, Boris was confident it would work.

By seven-thirty, all the preparations were complete. The pipelines were cleared for action, the leaf-builders stood at the ready in their forward positions, and stockpiles of cellulose, chlorophyll and other essential materials lay neatly distributed at key points in the system, available for instant transportation to the front line.

At eight o'clock, Mr. Lymer walked in. He glanced about, wagged a finger at the tomatoes saying, "Only four days to get ripe now! No slacking, my beauties!" and waddled out.

Boris peeped out from behind his canopy. When he was sure that Mr. Lymer had gone he whispered, "Stand by."

"Standing by" came the reply from the squadrons.

"And . . . forward!" said Boris.

At once the thick green trunks of the tomato plants began to stiffen as the fluids inside them started to run. Within minutes the highest leaf-bearing branches were stretching forward through the air, some pressing up towards the glass of the roof, others arching out in the direction of the door.

Stage Two was under way.

By nine o'clock the lettuces and parsley had woken up as well, and in spite of their thirst, began to talk.

"Something's wrong with the soil," said Andy. "I know it. We're definitely going to need help from outside."

Colin looked down from his shelf.

"I hope you're not thinking of us when you talk about help," he said. "We've made it perfectly clear that our hands are tied."

"You could at least try to think of something," said Esmeralda, "instead of just sitting up there."

"Think of something?" said Loretta. "Such as what?"

"I don't know. Anything. If you knew how horrible it feels, you'd – "

"I'll have you know, my girl," said Colin, "that we *do* know how it feels. Do you remember that terrible summer at the Assembly Hall, Loretta darling?"

"Do I just!" said Loretta. "That ghastly new caretaker. He didn't water us for two whole weeks! I thought I was done for. And you complain about a few hours! You wait till you've been dry for just *one* week, then come crying to me. Spoilt little hussy . . ."

"But we're so much smaller than you," cried Esmeralda. "We need water more often."

"Tripe," said Loretta. "Why don't you ask the tomatoes, or Gerald, for help? They're much closer to you."

"All right, I will! Boris!"

Boris's canopy moved up lazily.

"Yes?"

"Can't you help us? We're getting very dry here, and it looks as if it's going to be another hot day, and I don't think we'll be able to hold out unless we get some water."

Boris smiled regretfully. "I'm sorry, Esmeralda, but there's nothing I can do. Mr. Lymer's the one with the water."

"But Boris, we're old friends! We're your neighbours!"

"We didn't ask you to come and share our soil," said Boris. "In fact, we were against the idea from the beginning. You and your kind drink our water, you guzzle our minerals, you get in our way, you clog up our breathing space – in fact you're a pain in the neck! Now if you'll excuse me, I'm extremely busy."

39

With that the canopy dropped and Boris was hidden from view.

"Swine!" said Esmeralda. She felt like weeping, but she was so dry that no tears would come.

Eric turned to Gerald.

"Gerald, have you got any ideas . . . ? Gerald?"

"Hang on a moment."

Gerald was eavesdropping on a conversation that was taking place between two earthworms down among his roots.

"Which way are you going?" asked one of them.

"Up towards the lettuces," said the other.

"I've just come from there. Terrible."

"Why's that?"

"It's a jungle. You can't see your way for roots. Do you know, its taken me over two hours to get here?"

"From over there? Go on! You're winding me up."

"No! I swear it. I've been twisting and turning through that lot like a flippin' corkscrew."

"Whose roots are they?"

"The tomatoes'!"

"You *are* winding me up! What's a tomato root doing out here?"

"Don't ask me. All I know is, it's not making my job any easier. Anyone'd think we go round aerating the soil for fun. Ah well, I'd better slither off. The wife's doing mud stew for supper, and I'm already late."

"OK. See you around."

"So long."

The worms wriggled away.

"Well, well, well," said Gerald to himself. "So that's what the tomatoes are up to."

He turned to Eric. "Listen," he said. "I think I can explain what's happened, though that doesn't mean I can do anything to stop it. You are the victims of a nasty plot. Your water is being stolen by the tomatoes, whose roots have crept in among your own so that they can get it before you do. From the way Boris is speaking it's pretty clear that he's their leader, and I shouldn't think he intends to stop there. He probably wants to be everyone else's leader too, whether they like it or not. I wish I could see some way of helping you, but for the moment I can't. Unless Mr. Lymer intervenes, I think we shall all suffer. We may even die."

No one spoke. The plants gazed in fear at Boris's fat and glossy squadrons, his huge dangling bunches of tough green tomatoes. Not long ago they had laughed at the tomatoes' stupidity. Now they trembled at the thought of the limitless cruelty they could inflict.

"Have I got it about right, Boris?" asked Gerald.

Boris's canopy twitched. He appeared, half hidden by leaves.

"My plans will become clear in the fullness of time," he said. Then his leaves twitched again, and he was gone.

CHAPTER EIGHT

Colin and Loretta, Fred and his family of geraniums, and Gilbert, the cactus, were all secretly
relieved when they heard what Gerald said. A
disease is something vicious and invisible – it can
strike at any time and from any quarter, but a plot
by the tomatoes seemed much less sinister. From
the safety of their position on the shelves, they
looked down at the tomato beds and said to themselves. "Well, it's a shame, but at least we'll be all
right. There's nothing the tomatoes can do to us!"

And so they set their minds at rest and spread
themselves out for a nice day's sunbathing.

At four o'clock came the first hint that something
was wrong. A shadow moved across the sun.

"Probably a cloud," said Gilbert. "You never get
a full afternoon's sun in this place."

"Ah! A little welcome shade!" said Fred.

But the shade grew deeper, and did not pass as a
cloud would.

Loretta, who loved the sun, began to feel chilly.
She looked up to the sky, and gasped with fright.
Spread against the glass of the greenhouse roof,

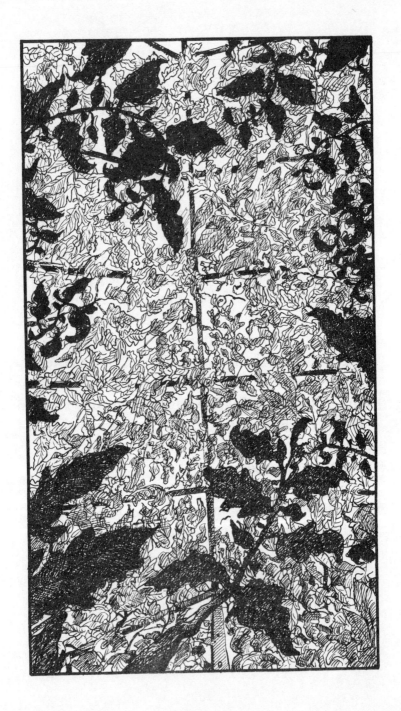

blocking out the light, was a thick and hairy mat of leaves. A glance along the branches told her instantly whose leaves they were.

"Colin," she said, "look! Our light's gone."

"What!" cried Colin, and looked up.

He was furious.

"This is a disgrace! What do you think you're doing? Fred! Gilbert! Look at this. It's an invasion!"

Fred and Gilbert also looked up. Then, looking down again, they saw that the light all around them, instead of being clear and bright as it normally was, had turned a thick, dark, muddy green. They knew very well what that meant. A plant needs light just as much as it needs water. Without either of them it will die.

Fred gulped. He decided he must speak out.

"Boris, I should like a word."

The canopy did not move.

"Boris . . . ? I say, Boris!"

Slowly the canopy lifted.

"What is it?" said Boris.

"I should like to make a complaint. Your friends and relations are blocking our light."

"Bad luck!"

"Bad luck! Is that all you're going to say?"

"Yes."

"But you'll destroy us!"

"Too bad."

"Boris, I can't believe you mean that. That is a vicious, unpleasant – "

45

"Fred," said Gerald, "don't waste your breath. The more nasty names you call him the better he feels."

"Well, what are we supposed to do?" shrieked Loretta. "Just sit here and accept it?"

"You told Esmeralda to do that."

"Well, I . . . I thought she was making a fuss about nothing."

"Was she?"

"No," Loretta sobbed.

"All right. Now, as I said, don't waste your breath complaining or crying or talking to Boris. Instead, you must try to think of ways to stop him."

Boris sniggered.

"You won't stop me," he said. "Not even Lymer can stop me now! I've got a plan that'll knock Lymer for six. Once he's out of the way, I shall finish off in here and we'll power out through that door like greased lightning and enslave the world. You can do all the thinking you like. It won't get you anywhere!"

"What do you mean when you say 'finish off in here'?" asked Fred.

"I mean that you lot – you useless, whining load of parasites – will be killed. We have no further use for you."

"Mr. Lymer won't allow it!" said Fred.

"Oh yes he will. When he gets a taste of the treatment I've got in store for him, he'll leave us well alone! Or he'll go the same way as you!"

*

At eight o'clock, Mr. Lymer walked into the green-house. Even though it was still light outside, he could barely see in there.

"Dear, oh dear!" he said. "What's going on in here? I don't like the look of this one little bit."

He switched on the light.

"Oh no! It's my tomatoes! Look at all these leaves! It won't help you get ripe, you know. I'll have to do something about it . . . " He looked at his watch. "But not tonight. I'm busy writing my acceptance speech for the first prize at the Agricultural Display. Heh-heh-heh. Still, I'd better give you your water for now . . . "

He picked up his watering-cans and dipped them into the tank. Air gulped and bubbled out of them as the water gurgled in. The plants cheered up at the sound. Even the lettuces and parsley looked forward to getting a few drops which might just escape the greedy tomatoes.

As he watered, Mr. Lymer noticed the tired, dry look of the lettuces and parsley, and gave them a little extra, not suspecting that he might as well have drunk it himself for all the good it would do them.

And sure enough, as he passed on, the water sank straight through the earth, into the waiting roots of the tomatoes. The other plants got nothing.

Mr. Lymer finished his rounds and switched off the light. At once the greenhouse was plunged into darkness.

*

47

Gerald looked out at the vegetable garden, and watched the light fade from the sky. As the darkness deepened, he noticed it was different from the dark inside. It wasn't gloomy or close; it was open, crossed by winds, lit by the stars. He wished he could escape – or, even better, smash through the walls of the greenhouse so that everyone could escape. After all, what was the place for? It was meant to protect the plants from dangers outside, but instead it shut them all in with worse dangers of their own.

He thought back with regret to the time of stories and songs. At this hour of the night everyone would be listening to Colin and Loretta crooning hits from old musicals, or Gilbert's weird tales of witches and lost gold, or Boris's wonderful jokes. Why had things changed? What was so attractive about squadrons and shouting and plans? Were the tomatoes actually *happier* now? It seemed to Gerald that something good had been thrown away for the sake of a mad and poisonous dream.

He listened to the sounds of the greenhouse. Someone was snuffling in his sleep. A tomato, fat with fluid, groaned and changed position on its stem. Water dripped into the tank. Gerald sighed, and allowed himself to wander off into a sad and troubled sleep.

CHAPTER NINE

Early next morning, when the sun had barely climbed over the hedge, Mr. Lymer walked in. His face was serious. In his right hand was a glinting pair of secateurs.

"All right, my beauties, we'll have to see to this leaf business. It won't do, you know. Oh no, indeed it won't."

He reached up to a long tomato branch and snipped through it. Then he did the same to another, and then another. The tomatoes, who were still half asleep, jumped with fright. The other plants saw what was happening and, thinking their luck had turned, cried out, "Lymer to the rescue! Yippee!"

But Boris was already in action.

"Squadrons," he growled. "Don't panic! Close eyes and prepare to commence night-time breathing. Stand by!"

"Standing by."

"And . . . blow!"

Suddenly there was a loud hiss as thousands of

tiny jets opened up on the leaves of the tomatoes and sprayed a bitter gas into the air. Mr. Lymer coughed, gasped, dropped his secateurs and stumbled out of the greenhouse, his mouth gaping, his chest heaving desperately.

Outside the door, he fell to his knees, tried to crawl a few feet, and collapsed.

"We've done it!" shouted Boris. "Lymer is beaten. He's gone! Three cheers! Hip hip . . . "

"Hurrah!"

"Hip hip . . . "

"Hurrah!"

"Hip hip . . . "

"Hurrah!"

The other plants were astounded. Boris had boasted that he would drive Mr. Lymer away, and he'd actually done it. However crafty Mr. Lymer might be, it seemed that Boris could go one better. Even Gerald was impressed. Boris might be cruel; he might even be mad; but his military planning was magnificent.

It was all so simple. First the root march under the soil to cut off the water supply. Then the foliage extension plan to cut off the light. And now the poison gas trick to cut off the air. Any plant could do it. It was just a matter of switching from its day-time breathing cycle to its night-time cycle, puffing out clouds of carbon dioxide, which human beings can't breathe. And since the "lungs" of a plant are in its leaves, Boris and the tomatoes, with all their new leaves, were in a position to produce as much carbon dioxide as they liked. No wonder Mr. Lymer was gasping.

The plants all watched him with different hopes as he lay on the grass outside. The tomatoes wished him dead, while the others prayed for him to come storming back in and take a terrible revenge on the evil tomato army.

51

Slowly, coughing, with a dazed look in his eyes, he got to his feet, and moved unsteadily towards the door again.

"Stand by!" called Boris.

"Standing by," the tomatoes replied.

Mr. Lymer stepped into the greenhouse and bent down for his secateurs. He looked about him for a moment, but suddenly his expression changed. He frowned, coughed, and leaned heavily on one of the shelves. His face was pale.

"God, I feel terrible," he said. Then he slipped the secateurs into his pocket, turned, and shuffled away.

Pandemonium broke out among the tomatoes. They cheered, and roared, and whooped, and laughed, shouting "Victory!" and "Death to Lymer!" and "Boris rules OK!"

Meanwhile, shut out from the high spirits and the celebrations, Gerald, Fred, Gilbert, Colin and Loretta, and all the wretchedly dried up lettuces and parsley, dropped their heads and let the gloom that was all around them flood into their hearts.

CHAPTER TEN

Two days passed. No one came to the greenhouse. The door stayed open day and night. Once in a while, birds would appear on the threshold, and hop curiously in to see what was around to eat. But just a few seconds in that dark, fetid air was enough to send them hopping out again.

Now, with no one watering them, all the plants became dry. Even Gerald, whose roots were long and deep, felt thirsty. With thirst came silence – hours of it – no more jokes, or songs, or opinions, just a long and horrible waiting. Outside they could hear the breeze ruffling the leaves of the trees, they could hear the birds chatter and sing, but they always came back to that silence.

Even the tomatoes were depressed. Although they were so bloated with water that they could have lived quite easily for many more days without help, they couldn't stop themselves wondering what exactly Boris had in mind if no one should ever water them again. And so a group of tomatoes raised the subject with him.

Boris sensed their unease, but, as with every other problem that had come up so far, he had a plan for it.

"So you want to know what we're going to do for water now that Lymer's gone for good?"

"Yes please, Boris."

"Well, I wasn't going to show you this scheme until tomorrow, but . . . if you insist . . . I suppose we could just about bring forward the grand unveiling by twenty-four hours . . . "

"Grand unveiling?"

"Yes! Why not? Gentlemen, cast your eyes at the water-tank, and keep them fixed there. In a moment you will see a phenomenon that you would never have believed possible . . . "

Every tomato turned to look. Within seconds, the soil around the water tank began to move. It swelled as if something were pushing from underneath. Suddenly, the surface broke, and a white, worm-like thing pushed up, quickly followed by others.

"Roots!" whispered the tomatoes.

They watched in growing amazement as more and more of the roots sprouted from the soil and began to snake up the side of the water tank. Before long they had reached the rim, they were curling over it, and dipping down towards the surface of the water. Then suddenly they were in, and at once they began pumping the water back. As the tomatoes felt their pipelines filling again, they gave a great shout of joy and called for Boris to speak.

This, as always, Boris was most willing to do.

"Gentlemen," he proclaimed, "this, which you see before you, is your lifeline: I built it myself with the help of my private team of root cells, as a surprise and as a gift, not only to you, but to all tomatoes all over the world! With the water from this tank, which is endlessly replenished from rain falling into the gutters of the greenhouse, we will fuel our conquest – not only of this greenhouse, not only of this vegetable garden, but of the whole earth! Nothing can stop us now. We are supreme! So never doubt and never fear, for Boris has a plan for everything! Boris will prevail!"

The tomatoes, liking the sound of this phrase, at once picked it up and made it their slogan, repeating it again and again.

"Boris will prevail! Boris will prevail! Boris will prevail!"

And the chanting, and the drinking, and the shouting, and the speeches, went on well into the night.

Finally, when everyone was hoarse and their excitement played out, they slept.

The night passed, followed by another long day of heat, and silence, and waiting. By evening, the tomatoes were starting to feel ever so slightly restless again. They knew it was wrong, but somehow they couldn't help feeling that, well, life could be a bit more *entertaining*. Conquest was very important, of course; it was thrilling while you were actually *doing* it, but it didn't give you very much to do in between times.

Dave (now an anonymous member of Typhoon Squadron) turned to Chris (who was in Thunderbolt) and whispered, "Hey, Chris!"

"Sssh!" said Chris. "That's not my name any more."

"I know," said Dave, "but I can't call you anything else, can I? I mean 'third tomato from the left on the fifth bunch from the top of Thunderbolt Squadron' is a bit of a mouthful, isn't it?"

"What do you want?"

"I was just wondering what you're thinking."

"Nothing in particular. How about you?"

"I'm thinking something that I probably shouldn't be thinking."

"What's that?"

"Can I trust you?"

"Of course you can."

"You won't tell anyone else?"

"No. I promise. Word of honour."

"I'm thinking that I miss the old days."

"Dave, you fool! Stop it! Boris'll kill you if he finds out."

"I know, but I can't stop myself remembering. I mean we had fun, didn't we? There used to be laughter and things to talk about. What do we do now?"

"We prevail."

"All right, we prevail. And what do we do *after* we've prevailed?"

"We prevail some more."

"Exactly! That's all we ever do, night and day. Apart from drinking, which I'm heartily sick of as well."

"Dave, listen to me. I know what you mean. Sometimes it can get to everyone, even a tomato . . ."

"What do you mean '*even*' a tomato? Tomatoes like having fun! We don't like sitting around – "

"Will you please listen? You may have doubts. We all do. It's natural. But you must learn to resist them. Not just for your own sake, but for the sake of our glorious future as tomatoes. Take my advice and keep quiet, or I'm telling you there'll be trouble. In fact, if someone's heard us talking like this . . . " – Chris looked suspiciously around – "there'll be trouble anyway. You'd better watch your step."

"Don't you think anyone else feels like I do?"

"If they do they've had the good sense to keep it to themselves."

Dave felt puzzled and hurt. Couldn't you talk to your friends anymore?

Just then a tomato next to him nudged him and whispered, "I agree with you, Dave, I'm bored stiff. So's the bloke next to me. But *please, please* keep it quiet. There are informers around. Boris gets to know everything."

"Why shouldn't he know what we think? He's the one who got us into this state, isn't he? It can't do any harm if he . . . "

"It can do a lot of harm. I've heard Boris has got all kinds of horrible punishments lined up for anyone who gets in his way."

"What sort of punishments?"

"Strangling, disembowelling, stifling, eating alive by ants . . . "

"Ugh! Stop! That's revolting."

"It's what I've heard tell . . . "

Dave was beginning to feel weak. "I think I will keep quiet from now on," he said.

"I should," said his neighbour.

Dave reflected uncomfortably that, compared to being strangled, sitting around feeling bored might not be so bad after all.

CHAPTER ELEVEN

Boris heard every word that Dave spoke. He was angry, of course – furious even – but he managed to fight back an impulse to smash him to the ground. His thoughts moved cunningly on to the effect of such an action. Dave – even though that was not officially his name now – was a popular tomato, always liked and respected for "having a go". If Boris destroyed him, Dave's friends might get angry. They might even plan some kind of revenge. The last thing Boris wanted was a fight in the ranks of his army.

He also knew that Dave and his two neighbours were not the only tomatoes who felt restless. He even felt that way himself. It irritated him. It was as if some part of him was itching, but he couldn't find the spot to scratch it.

What really niggled him, though, was that he had no plan. He hadn't seen this problem coming.

He decided to improvise. This was not something he was good at, but he had no choice. A bored army means trouble. He would have to entertain them.

So he gave a great shout. "All right, you soppy

lot! Off your backs! We're going to have a discussion. A sing-song. A good time will be had by
all!"

There were groans and unhappy murmurs all
round.

"What!" exclaimed Boris to his squadrons,
"you're not tired are you? There's a lot more to do
before we conquer the earth, you know. You're
getting soft. You're going all weak and marsh-
mallowy. You've had it too good. I'll have to
toughen you up!"

"No!" pleaded the squadrons, perking up instantly, for they knew what "toughening up"
meant: exercises all night long, with Boris shouting "Oxygen! In, out, in, out, in, out. Carbon dioxide! In, out, in, out, in, out. Oxygen! In, out . . . "
with press-ups, squat-thrusts, knee-bends (particularly painful for tomatoes), burpees and all kinds
of other horrible exertions, on and on without a
break until the first streaks of dawn appeared over
the prickly hedge.

"At your service!" they cried, as cheerily as they
could.

"That's better," said Boris, who loved the word
"service". "Now, let's have a nice brisk discussion."

"What about?" asked the leader of the Edelweiss
Squadron.

"About the future," said Boris. "About our
plans."

"Well, as I see it," said the leader of the Famine

61

Squadron, "first, there's all the other plants to kill, and from then on . . . well, it's the outside world, I suppose."

"Obviously!" said Boris impatiently. "But I want to know more. I want to imagine our conquest of the earth, I want to hear about the battles with trees and insects, the victories over men and monkeys. I want to know the whole thing!"

There was silence among the tomatoes. Few of them had thought so far ahead. And those that had were secretly afraid. They could see the tall oaks and poplars through the glass; they saw that they were actually rather huge, and probably very strong, and some of them doubted whether even Boris himself was cunning enough to defeat them.

It was then that they heard, from behind them, a voice that had not spoken for many days. It was Gerald.

"Listen to me, Boris, you and all your army. I've been watching you, and listening to you, for a while now. I know what you're up to, and quite frankly I'm not very impressed. I've lived a lot longer than you have. I've seen something of the world. Let me say this: you know nothing – absolutely nothing. You can sit here and make all the plans you like, but I can tell you now you won't get past the greenhouse door . . . Do you know what country we're in?"

"Borisland!" cried a junior officer in the War Squadron.

"Rubbish!" said Gerald. "We're in England. And do you know why we're in a greenhouse?"

No one replied. They had never given that much thought.

"I'll tell you. Because in England the climate is too cold for tomatoes to grow outdoors. In summer, OK, you *might* survive. But come winter, with the snow, and frost, and ice, you'll die like flies. You haven't got a hope. And don't believe anyone who says you have."

The tomatoes were shocked. None of them knew what to say. They had an awful itchy feeling that Gerald might be right. On the other hand, he might be wrong . . . They just couldn't tell.

They turned to Boris, who was staring at Gerald with loathing in his eyes.

"Do you imagine," he purred, "that I haven't thought of that? Do you really imagine that I'm so stupid, so cowardly, so ignorant as to forget the English winter? There's something you ought to know, Gerald, something important, that'll do you a lot of good, and that is BORIS HAS A PLAN FOR EVERYTHING! BORIS WILL PREVAIL! Got it?"

Gerald looked straight back at him.

"All right, what's your plan for the winter?"

"That," said Boris, "is a secret."

"Tell us! Tell us!" yelled his squadrons.

"SILENCE!" screamed Boris. "I shall tell no one my plan until the time draws near. Have I ever let you down?"

"No," said the squadrons.

"And I won't let you down over this. But beware, a greater enemy than the winter lurks here among us. That enemy is Gerald the vine! He may be old, but he's certainly not wise. He's a fool! He's weak! He's all gaga! He'll be dribbling from his mouth next week!"

The tomatoes all laughed loudly. Good old Boris! He had an answer for everything.

Gerald waited till the laughter stopped, then said, "Boris, you say you're going to conquer the earth. Can you tell me why? Here are all these plants dying around you. Why are you doing it? What have they done to you?"

"They have stood in my way!" cried Boris. "And I shall conquer the earth because I want to be great!"

"But *why*?" Gerald insisted.

"Because that's the way I am!"

"All right, let me ask you another question. Do you like being hated?"

"I'm not hated."

"You are. What do you think those poor lettuces over there feel about you? Wouldn't you hate someone who was killing you horribly and slowly?"

"I don't care what they think! I have my faithful squadrons. They are all the friends and admirers I need."

"Are you sure they're faithful, Boris? How do you know there isn't another Boris among them, another tomato who wants to be great, who's already plotting behind your back, and who one day will push you off your stalk like a rotten apple?"

Boris's left eye began to twitch uncontrollably, as it always did when he thought about nasty things like death, or failure, or being picked. But he spoke out boldly.

"There is only one Boris, and I am supreme! No one challenges me . . . But let me prove it. Squadrons! Is there anyone here who thinks Gerald may be right?"

All the tomatoes looked round at each other. None dared to speak.

"Come on!" said Boris. "Don't be shy! Gerald can be quite persuasive when he wants to be. There must be at least one of you who thinks that he's said just one sensible thing tonight."

The two tomatoes next to Dave in the Typhoon Squadron glanced at each other and nodded. Timidly they each raised a leaf.

"There you are," said Gerald.

"Absolutely," said Boris suavely, then yapped "Get them!"

Suddenly the two tomatoes felt the most horrible twisting and pulling in their insides. For a moment they felt sick, then realized with terror that their juice was being sucked out at terrific speed. They felt dizzy, violently ill – then blackness.

Within seconds they were hanging from their stalks like limp balloons, dead.

"Thank you," said Boris to the Typhoon's security section, who were now fatter than ever and panting heavily.

"So you see, Gerald," he went on, "there's no problem about rebels. Every tomato is a friend and admirer – those that aren't don't last long."

Gerald said nothing. Dave trembled on his stem.

"No more questions?" asked Boris, sensing yet another victory.

"I have a feeling," said Gerald softly, "a very strong feeling, right down along my roots, and all the way up my trunk, and through to the tips of my leaves, that you, Boris, are going to come to a very . . . *very* . . . nasty end."

And as he said those words, with slow and sinister confidence, all the tomatoes – even Boris – felt cold shivers run right along them. It was as if winter had already arrived.

Suddenly Boris didn't feel like talking any more. He certainly didn't want a sing-song. He decided to ignore Gerald's last remark and the fear that chilled his heart.

"End of discussion – time for sleep!" he announced, and snapped shut his eyes.

But he did not sleep. Behind his closed eyes, his brain was already working hard. Gerald was a danger to his plans. He was taking too long to die. He must be dealt with swiftly and ruthlessly.

A plan soon began to form in his mind.

CHAPTER TWELVE

As dawn broke the next day, Boris was up giving orders. His plan was ready. He had worked on it right through the night. All that was needed now was speed and surprise.

The tomatoes were unhappy to be woken up so early. They had grown accustomed to sleeping until noon, and several of them yawned loudly as Boris spoke. But the more he said, the more they began to feel once again the excitement that only Boris knew how to create.

"Today," said Boris solemnly, "is the big day. Today we burn our boats. From now on there can be no going back, no wavering, no regrets. We are going to break out of the greenhouse!"

The tomatoes were astonished.

"All of us?" asked one of the Scorpions.

"Not quite all," said Boris. "We will leave a caretaker squadron in charge here. They will keep the rest of us supplied with water and other essentials until such time as we have established a bridgehead in the vegetable garden. From there we

69

will move on to take over the rest of the earth. Any questions?"

"Yes, Boris. What about the question of winter?"

"Ah. So those two traitors I flushed out last night weren't the only ones who thought Gerald had a point?"

"No, Boris, I'm not saying he had a point . . . I'm just sort of . . . wondering."

"Just wondering, eh? Well just to stop anyone else wondering, I'll tell you. Somewhere – up beyond the prickly hedge – is the house where Lymer lives. My guess is, it's pretty snug and comfortable in there. Very suitable, in fact, as winter quarters for an army of tomatoes."

"You mean, we're going to live in a house for human beings?"

"Of course! We'll have log fires, roast chestnuts, hot spicy wine . . . the lot. And there, through the long frosty evenings, we can plan our campaign for the spring. How does that sound?"

"It sounds fantastic."

"Correct. But all that is still a very long way off. We're going to have to work hard to get there. There won't be a moment's slacking. You won't have time to get bored. It'll be non-stop action from now on in."

"That's fine by us!" said the tomatoes.

"It had better be! Now very shortly we shall set off. But first, there is some unfinished business. We must attend to it now, or it could ruin everything.

It's a matter of life or death . . . or, to be more precise, a matter of death. Gerald's death . . . "

Boris paused.

"Let me explain. The other plants are now so weak that nothing can save them. We have nothing to fear from them. I shall shortly be giving permission for a friendly contingent of fungus mould to move in and begin devouring them. *But* . . . unless Gerald is removed – and quickly! – we cannot even sleep safely at night, never mind think of conquering the earth. For you must realize that he is a threat – worse than that, he is a traitor! Only last night – and I blush to say this – I caught him trying to creep up on me and strangle me in the dark! So let us do away with niceties of conscience, let us be bold, let us give him a taste of his own treacherous medicine and strangle him now as he sleeps!"

"Yes! Let's do it!" cried the tomatoes. "Let's kill him!"

"That's the spirit!" said Boris. "But we must do it calmly and in the proper way. In my view it's a job for the roots. Anyone disagree?"

"No, Boris. It's definitely a job for the roots."

"Good. Now, I want all roots in the vicinity of Gerald's main stem to report to fruitquarters at once. Proceed, and await further orders."

The tomatoes went quickly into action, sending out messages, gauging distances, and consulting root maps. Very soon they had their results.

71

The leader of the Scorpion Squadron raised a leaf.

"Permission to report, Boris?" he said.

"Permission granted."

"The nearest roots belong to Stingray, Thunderbolt and Scorpion."

"Very well. Now listen carefully, all of you. Those roots, and those roots only, will march directly to the area where Gerald's roots come in to meet his main stem. No matter where his water comes from, it must all pass through that area. Once you have reached it, I want each root to advance on ONE of Gerald's roots and coil itself tightly round it several times. DON'T go for the main stem. It'll be too strong for you. But make sure you get EVERY ONE of the subsidiaries. Is that absolutely clear?"

"Yes, Boris."

"Right. That's the first stage. The second stage involves everyone. When you hear that all the roots are in place, that is to say, coiled round Gerald's roots, I want you to pump as much water as you can towards them. Pump for your life! The water will swell the coils round Gerald's roots, thus squeezing them horribly. Quite apart from the agony it will cause him, it'll certainly cut off his circulation below ground, all his systems will rapidly come to a halt, and he'll be dead within . . . ooh, ten minutes, at the most. At that point you can stop pumping, the mould boys will charge in, and

our greenhouse campaign will come to a trium-
phant end. From then on, the conquest of the earth
can begin! Are you ready?"

"Ready, Boris."

"Stand by!"

"Standing by!"

"Stingray, Thunderbolt and Scorpion roots,
quick march!"

This was what the tomatoes had been waiting
for! No more boredom, no more waiting! Action!
Root-to-root fighting! At last!

From Gerald's point of view, of course, things
were very far from pleasant. If you have ever
woken up to find a boa constrictor wrapped round
your legs, squeezing them so hard that you can
hear the bones crunch inside (and few who have
live to tell the tale), you will know exactly how he
felt. He woke up in a fit of excruciating pain. He
tried to squirm free, but the roots held him so
tight he could not budge by even a hair's breadth
to left or right. His eyes started to water. His
branches felt weak. His leaves drooped. He
could hardly breathe. His thoughts became
jumbled, falling over each other, tangling each
other up. He was confused, bewildered, desperate,
choking.

Through the fog in his eyes he could just see
Boris's leering face.

"Who's dying a nasty death now?" snarled Boris.

"Who's got all the clever ideas now? Who's not going to survive the winter now? Eh?"

Then Gerald heard Boris laugh. A vicious, bloodthirsty, sickening laugh that gurgled like water being swallowed by a drain. The other tomatoes joined in, adding their own stupid chorus of gurgles and gulps and hiccoughs, until it seemed to Gerald that his life itself was being sucked down a long, dark, twisting drainpipe, echoing endlessly away.

Then, all of a sudden, the laughter stopped. Gerald's roots were released. His thoughts began to unjumble themselves and vision drifted back into his eyes. There was the most extraordinary silence, as if time stood still. Was this it, he wondered? Was he dead?

A moment later he knew he was not, as the silence was broken – by one tense word.

"Lymer!"

Gerald glanced towards the door. There stood Mr. Lymer, his plump body a little slimmer, his ruddy face a little paler, but his black glittery eyes and wild eyebrows fiercer looking than ever before. Over his nose he held a folded handkerchief. In his right hand was a pair of secateurs. Behind him, ready to help, stood Mr. Cottle.

"Right, you lot," said Mr. Lymer with an unmistakable note of menace in his voice, "no more tricks this time! This is it!"

CHAPTER THIRTEEN

Suddenly, Boris was frantic.

"Look out! he shouted. "Lymer approaching with secateurs! Prepare to gas! Prepare to gas!"

The tomatoes, tired and breathing heavily from their efforts to strangle Gerald, were slow to respond.

"Forget Gerald!" cried Boris. "Prepare for night-time breathing! Switch over to CO_2! Stand by to blow!"

Cursing the sudden change of plan, the tomatoes clamped their eyes shut and did their best to obey. But Mr. Lymer was snipping fast. With every branch he cut off, the tomatoes lost hundreds of gas outlets, and one sunbeam after another jabbed into the gloom. Several tomatoes were slashed. It was looking bad . . .

Then Mr. Lymer faltered. He coughed, tried to breathe in, found he couldn't, and with panic darting in his eyes, ran stumbling out.

The tomatoes stopped blowing. They were shattered. Several were wounded. All were confused.

Cries of pain and fear, then complaints and accusations, began to fly.

"Oh!" groaned one tomato, "I've been cut!"

"Stop moaning," panted another, still out of breath.

"Why shouldn't I moan?" said the first one aggressively. "You would if you'd been cut."

"I wouldn't," said the other.

"Shut up both of you!" said a third. "If you want something to shout about, look at me."

They looked and saw that a ray of sun had picked him out and seemed to be pouring energy into him down its slope of burning light. The side of the tomato was on fire!

"I'm burning," said the tomato. "I'm turning red, I can't stop it, the sun's got right down into me and I can feel my innards turning yellow and orange! Help! Help!"

The other tomatoes were too horrified to help. They knew what the redness meant. It meant ripeness, being picked – then salad or soup, as Boris had said – in other words, the end! They sat still – no longer chattering or complaining, no longer thinking of victory, but waiting, in terror, for the sun.

Meanwhile Boris had lost his canopy in the attack, but he was very far from panicking. Instead he had made use of the confusion. He saw what had happened with the sunlight and could see the danger for himself. So he sent an order, quickly and without fuss, through the system. "All leaf-builders to Boris. All leaf-builders to Boris at once please." And they all came scurrying to see what he wanted.

"Build me a new canopy," he said, "fast! Right the way round."

And in a couple of minutes, leaves were sprouting all round Boris as the builders pushed and pumped and strained to get their canopy up.

"Faster!" shouted Boris, for he knew time was short. The builders worked even harder, grunting and heaving with effort.

Then Dave saw what Boris was doing. He snapped out of his trance of fear and called to the builders.

"Hey, come on, do some patching up over here, against the glass! Then all of us will be protected, not just Boris."

Other tomatoes turned to look, and they too called to the builders to come to the glass.

"Stay here and I'll do anything for you, I'll make you rich, you can govern whole vegetable gardens, name your price – I'll pay it – but FINISH MY CANOPY!" yelled Boris.

"Come on, brothers," shouted all the tomatoes of the Typhoon and Cobra Squadrons together, "protect us all or we all die, you as well!"

The builders turned to Boris.

"It makes sense," they said. "None of us will survive if we don't help them."

"Nonsense!" said Boris. "I'll make sure you survive."

And the leaf-builders looked from Boris to the others, then to Boris again, then back to the others, to and fro like spectators at a tennis match, taking orders from each but not knowing whom to obey.

Suddenly, the argument amongst the tomatoes ceased, for as Mr. Lymer lay on the ground, gulping in the fresh air, his friend Mr. Cottle had picked up the secateurs and was striding ferociously into the greenhouse.

Boris shouted, "Human being! Carbon dioxide! Action stations!" adding a "Red Alert!" for good measure. "Squeeze!" he yelled, "Squeeeeeeeeze!"

The tomatoes shuddered with the effort of taking in and pushing out so much breath. But Mr. Cottle walked on, and brandishing his secateurs, snipped off leaf after leaf until the sun was pouring through in twenty different places. The tomatoes' Leaf Extension Plan, their great canopy against the sun, began to look more like a punctured old tea-strainer with every snip that he made. The tomatoes began to panic, they were out of breath, their leaves in shreds, they couldn't go on, and every moment new spears of sunlight were shooting eagerly in.

They were about to give up hope when suddenly Mr. Cottle too began to cough, turned his back, and staggered out.

The tomatoes stopped pumping. They stopped

everything. They hung there, stunned and horrified. Fifty wounds wept in silence as they tried to understand what had happened. They had never known such an attack, the cold steel blades slicing so fast through their stalks that they didn't even feel them. They shivered with fear at the memory; then shivered again as they saw the other enemy, sunbeams, gushing in to drown them in fire.

Then, one by one, they turned to Boris – for comfort, ideas, advice, anything to help them live on.

But Boris did not notice. As soon as the attack was over, he was back with the leaf-builders, ordering them to finish his canopy before it was too late. And the builders were pushing and straining and pumping, knowing they'd never get any peace until they'd finished the job for Boris. And as they built, they cursed him and all his plans to the ends of the earth and beyond.

CHAPTER FOURTEEN

The leaf-builders were not the only ones to curse Boris.

Dave, who was now sitting smack in the centre of a huge beam of sunlight, watched Boris carefully. He could feel the sun's warmth creeping through him, he could feel his insides starting to glow, and then, quite suddenly, to his amazement, he didn't mind. He had been dreading this moment for so long, yet now it had happened it wasn't nearly so bad as he'd imagined. In fact he liked the warmth. It felt good. It eased him inside. But he didn't like what Boris was doing.

"Boris!" he called.

"What do you want?" Boris answered.

"I'm wondering about something, and I expect the others are wondering about the same thing."

"Well, get on with it, I haven't got all day."

"I'm wondering why you've got all the leaf-builders still working for you, when you can see that you've lost the battle."

"I haven't lost. I never lose!"

"You have, Boris. We've all lost. And you're trying to save your skin by hiding behind your leaves. If you cared about us you'd send the leaf-builders to repair the damage – but you don't, you're thinking only of yourself."

"I'm not. I'm thinking of you – all of you. I'm making plans to save the day."

"It's too late for plans, Boris. If you're thinking of us, why are you hogging the leaf-builders? Tell us that. Why should we go red and be picked for salads and soup, while you stay green?"

"Because I'm your leader. If you die, someone must stay behind to carry on the good work, to lead a new generation to victory. That's why I must be protected . . . You hadn't thought of that, had you?"

The other tomatoes had not in fact thought of that, and Dave was rather stuck for a reply. He was just about to shout something terribly brave but not very clever, like "Who cares?" when Gerald spoke.

"Boris is right, you know," he said. There was a hush. "You have to think of the future."

"Thank you, Gerald!" said Boris. "It's nice to know there's someone around here with a bit of sense. Now as soon as the builders have finished my canopy they can move up and try . . . "

"Excuse me," said Gerald, "I haven't finished."

"Sorry! Do continue," said Boris.

"Thank you. The trouble is, Boris's plan for the future won't work; and he knows it – because, in spite of everything, he is a clever tomato. He's so clever that he's fooled you all with his lies. You see, the next generation will come, not from him, but from you, from the seeds that you carry; and none of you will survive to see them, because you must ripen and split open for the seeds to escape. If you don't die, no future tomatoes will live – it's as simple as that. Even Boris must die."

"Lies!" yelled Boris. "Treacherous lies!"

"They're not lies," said Gerald, "and you know it. Admit it . . . Go on, you've got nothing to lose."

"I've got my empire, my army to lose. I must remain alive to keep the sacred flame of . . . "

"Rubbish!" shouted Dave. "It's you or us. That's all you care about, and I vote you should go first!"

"You can't decide who goes first – only I can. And you'd better watch your tongue or . . . "

"All those who agree that Boris should go first, help me squeeze now!" cried Dave, and all the tomatoes in his squadron squeezed for all they were worth. Then one by one the other squadrons joined in, until they were all squeezing together – and all in the direction of Boris.

Boris managed to shout, "Don't be stupid, I'll kill . . . " before he felt a terrible pressure at the top of his head and the words turned to blocks of wood in his mouth. The pressure grew and grew, until it was so great that Boris couldn't move at all. His eyes and mouth stuck open wide, he was as rigid as a lump of stone.

How long could they keep it up? If he could hold out he'd come back and punish the lot of them with a new and even more cunning plan. He could see the tomatoes straining till their veins stood out like tree-roots. Who would weaken first? One or two others were already looking exhausted, ready to burst; he felt he would make it, he, Boris the Great, would battle on ... but then there was a sound that filled him with terror – a sound of tearing fibres. His stalk was coming unstuck! He tried to shout but he couldn't, the fibres were loosening, and suddenly WHOOSH! he was shooting through the air at a fantastic speed. He was heading for the glass!

There was a terrific smash. Mr. Lymer and Mr. Cottle looked up, and ducked as a dark green object punched through the greenhouse glass and flew at them like a cannon ball. Then they picked themselves up and ran into the greenhouse to see what had happened. All they could see at the far end was a spray of water so thick that it hid all the plants from view. Across it the sun made a rainbow. They went closer, and the spray struck them in their faces. A few steps further on, shielding their eyes with their hands, they could see that the water was coming from a tomato plant – or seemed to be.

Mr. Cottle tapped Mr. Lymer's shoulder and pointed to a tomato near them – it was shrinking before their eyes! Then they glanced at the soil. It was rippling, and here and there white roots would

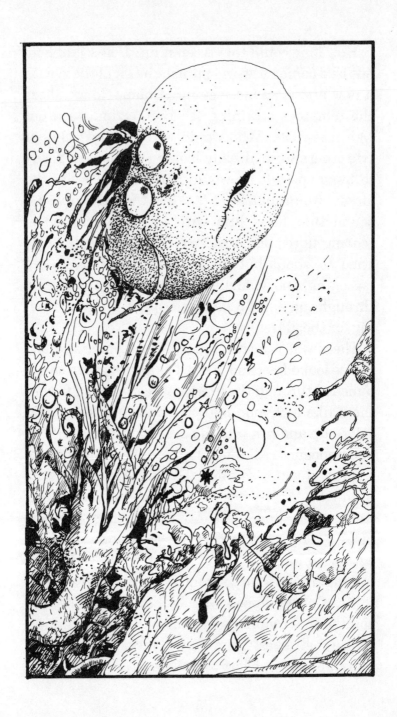

suddenly shoot out and then whip back under the surface again. The roots were shrinking too!

Unheard by the two men, Dave cried out, "Stop!"

The spray, however, went on as fast as ever.

"Stop!" he cried again. "For God's sake stop!"

"I can't" shouted a watery voice.

"Neither can I," gurgled another.

"Can't anyone stop?" came a much weaker cry.

There was no reply.

"Are you there?" asked Dave. "What's happened? Oh, I feel awful! I'm blacking out . . . "

Then there was silence. The spray began to slow down, and the rainbow faded away. At last there was only a trickle, and the two men, drenched through, could see now that it came from one stalk that hung beneath a canopy of dripping leaves . . .

"That must have been the one that flew out!" Mr. Cottle said, and went off to investigate.

Mr. Lymer stood where he was, stupefied at this scene of wreckage. The tomatoes – his bumper crop – were hanging in drooping, wrinkled bunches like limp green rubber gloves. There was water everywhere, streaming down the glass, dripping off the plants, trickling down his forehead and cheeks. It even squelched in his shoes.

From outside, he heard Mr. Cottle calling. He walked out into the bright sun and saw his friend standing over the compost heap, beckoning.

"Come here!" he said. "Look at this."

Mr. Lymer found himself looking down at a

gigantic green tomato, streaked with black, its glossy skin in shreds.

"I recognize that one," he said, shaking his head. "That was my champion."

Mr. Cottle put his arm on Mr. Lymer's shoulder.

"I'm sorry," he said. "Look, I know it's no consolation, but I'm sure that if that tomato had ripened you'd have easily won first prize at the Agricultural Display."

"I know," said Mr. Lymer sadly. "That's the worst part about it."

"Oh come on, old chap," said Mr. Cottle, "it's not the end of the world! Something went a little bit wrong, that's all. To my mind, anyway, you've proved that you can breed tomatoes like no one else on earth. And that's something to be proud of."

Mr. Lymer smiled. He decided to invite Mr. Cottle to breakfast, and as he did so he realized that he hadn't asked anyone to breakfast – or lunch, or dinner or even tea – for as long as he could remember.

"Thank you," said Mr. Cottle, "that'd be very nice."

And so they set off for the house.

CHAPTER FIFTEEN

From inside the devastated greenhouse, Gerald watched the two men disappear. Then he looked at the soaking, bedraggled mess around him. The lettuces and parsley were splayed limply about. The tomatoes, Boris's fierce killer squadrons, were all dead – their stems twisted, their leaves shrivelled, their great pipeline of roots tangled and burst. And what of Fred and Gilbert? Colin and Loretta? Had they survived?

Gerald cast an anxious eye over them. Fred was pale and yellow; Gilbert's normally firm skin seemed soft and sickly; Colin and Loretta looked healthy enough, but neither spoke nor stirred.

"Colin," said Gerald. "Colin!"

There was no reply.

"Colin . . . ? Are you all right . . . ? Speak to me . . . "

Another voice joined Gerald's.

"Colin, you lazy old clump of greenery – wake up! Gerald's calling."

"Loretta!" cried Gerald. "You're all right!"

"Yes! What about you?"

"Recovering."

"Recovering? From what?"

"The tomatoes tried to strangle me. Very nearly succeeded too."

"My dear, that must have been absolutely ghastly."

"It wasn't much fun. How's Colin?"

"Oh he's all right. Aren't you, Col . . . ? Col?"

Loretta lifted one of her fronds and gave Colin a powerful swipe.

"Colin, you layabout!" she boomed.

If Colin was in a weak state already, thought Gerald, that blow might well have finished him off altogether. But Colin opened his eyes, blinked, and asked, "What's up?" as if nothing was wrong at all.

"Are you all right?" asked Gerald.

"Me? All right? Of course I am . . . I say, what's going on? It looks as if a bomb's hit the place. Is everyone OK?"

"The tomatoes aren't. Nor are the lettuces or parsley. I don't know about Fred or Gilbert."

"Fred," said a dry, but unmistakable voice, "is A-OK. No great problems here. A bit yellow round the gills, but I'll be right as rain in a couple of days . . . I say, talking of rain, what's happened to Gilbert?"

All eyes turned to the sad-looking cactus, dripping wet in his pot on the shelf.

"Gilbert," said Fred, "how goes it old amigo? Are you all right?"

Gilbert showed no signs of life.

"Oh, I do hope the poor dear's not dead," said Loretta. "I'd miss him hugely."

"Sssh!" said Fred. "Listen."

There was a faint muttering coming from Gilbert's general direction. Snatches of words could be heard from time to time, mixed up with strange moans.

"That was bad," said the muttering voice. "Very, very bad . . . ooh, o-ohh, ohhh, oh-ohh . . . very very bad."

"What was bad?" asked Loretta in a whisper. "Do you mean what we've all been through?"

"Bad to let them die."

"Bad to let who die, Gilbert? Who? Surely not the tomatoes?"

"I think he's raving," said Loretta. "He must have caught a fever."

"He's a bit loopy at the best of times," said Fred.

Gilbert went on, "Poor Esmeralda, poor Eric, poor Andy . . . "

A thin, high voice interrupted him.

"Hang on a sec, Gilbert, I'm not dead! Nor's Andy."

Gilbert stopped muttering at once.

"Who's that?" he cried.

"Esmeralda."

"Esmeralda! I don't believe it! You're alive!"

"Just about, thanks to that lovely shower of rain."

"Yeah, that was really nice," said another voice.

"Ron!" exclaimed Gilbert. "You too! You're OK?"

Ron gave him the thumbs-up.

"I'm OK. Battered, lost height and speed, but still cruising along. How about you, Eric?"

"I'm right there with you," said Eric.

Gilbert was jubilant. "This is great! Fantastic! We must celebrate!"

"How shall we celebrate?" asked Fred.

"What about a song?" said Loretta. *"Tiptoe Through The Tulips?"*

"No!" said Fred. "We need something stirring – something special to mark the occasion. Got any ideas, Gerald?"

"Well, as it happens, I've cooked up something that might just do the trick."

"Let's hear it!" said Colin.

"Really?" said Gerald. "It's not terribly good you know."

"Never mind!" cried the others. "Sing it to us."

"All right," said Gerald. "It's called *The Ballad of Boris the Tomato.*"

Gerald cleared his throat, and began to sing in a mellow, tuneful voice.

BALLAD OF BORIS THE TOMATO

'Twas on the fifteenth of July –
The sun was burning hot –

That Boris, the tomatoes' lord,
Drew up his fiendish plot:

The roots would march beneath the soil,
The branches cross the sky,
The leaves would blow in Lymer's face
And foul his air supply!

The wind sprang up, the rain lashed down,
Lightning scarred the night,
The thunder roared, and Boris sent
His squadrons off to fight.

Their enemies were all the world,
All plants and beasts and trees,
All insects, fishes, birds and men,
All mountains and all seas.

But first they had to subjugate
The merry greenhouse mob.
"A piece of cake!" they thought, and yet
It proved no easy job.

For just when they were on the point
Of carrying the day,
Lymer came back, the branches got hacked,
And Boris was blown away!

Oh hey diddle dum and hey diddle doo,
And hey diddle doo-di-ay,
Lymer came back, the branches got hacked,
And Boris was blown away!

"Hurrah!" cried Gilbert. "Bravo!" and everyone cheered and clapped and said it was easily the best song they'd ever heard in all their lives. Gerald shook his head. "No," he said, "it really isn't very good. Especially the last verse. I made that up in a bit of a hurry."

"Nonsense!" said Fred. "It's the best verse of the lot. Besides, it's the only one that makes sense!"

"Hey, why don't you teach us the song?" said Eric. "I think it would do very well as our greenhouse anthem."

"Hear, hear!" said Colin.

Gerald felt embarrassed. "No," he said. "I don't think so."

"Sing it again!" said Loretta. "Encore!"

So at last Gerald was persuaded to sing it again, and then again, and indeed several times more after that until everyone knew it by heart.

While this noisy celebration went on, Boris was lying, wounded, on the compost heap, with rotting egg-shells and cabbage-leaves for company. A warm, steamy smell of decay rose all around him from his soggy bed of mouldering vegetables.

Terrible bolts of pain shot through him, twisting and burning his insides. Yet still he found strength to fix the greenhouse in the furious glare of his one remaining eye and shout, "I'll be back, you yellow-bellied lot! You haven't seen the last of me! I'll come

back and I'll take such a horrible revenge that you'll . . . you'll . . . "

But suddenly he stopped. A blackbird had landed on the grass nearby, with a hungry look in its eye that Boris didn't much care for.

"Don't you come near me!" he snarled. "You'll regret it!"

But the blackbird came closer.

"I'm Boris!" he yelled. "You can't touch me. I'm the Supreme, the . . . "

A second blackbird appeared, looking just as hungry as the first.

"What do you think?" asked the second.

"Looks pretty tasty," said the first. "Shall we give it a go?"

"All right."

Boris didn't have time to object. He could only gasp with surprise as the birds plunged their beaks deeply into him and began to eat.

A crowd of starlings fluttered down to finish off the job.

When the feast was over, the birds dispersed. Nothing but a few curls of skin remained. Boris, champion of the tomatoes, fiendish military planner, self-styled conqueror of the world, was dead.